# The Clumsy Crocodile

## Felicity Everett

Adapted by Rebecca Treays

## Illustrated by Alex de Wolf

Reading Consultant: Alison Kelly
Roehampton University of Surrey

# Contents

# Chapter 1

# Everglades

Cassy Green was on her way to work. It was the very first day of her new job.

She was going to work at
Everglades, the biggest and
best store in town.

It sold things you just couldn't buy anywhere else. So, when Cassy got a job there, she was as pleased as punch.

• Toy Department
• China Department
• Exotic Pet Department
• Robot Department
• Luxury Goods Department
• Food Hall

First, Cassy was sent to work in the China Department. After only ten minutes, she had sold sixty cups and saucers to a very rich lady. She was doing well.

Cassy packed the china carefully into a box. She was as gentle as a crocodile can be, but maybe just a little slow. The lady began to get impatient.

Cassy quickly tied a big bow
on the box. She didn't want the
lady to be cross, not her very first
customer. But as Cassy picked up
the box, disaster struck!

She'd packed it upside down.
Sixty cups and saucers smashed
onto the floor.

The customer stamped her foot
angrily and left.

Next Cassy was sent to the Toy Department. She hoped there was less to break. She didn't want any more accidents.

"I must put this ball away," she thought. "Someone could trip over it and have a bad fall."

But as she bent down, her
tail swung out behind her. The
Toytown Express was knocked
right off its rails.

So she was sent to the Food Hall.
But there, things went from bad
to worse.

Cassy tripped over a stool. A
bowl of salad flew into the air
and landed...

...on Ernest Everglade's head.
Ernest Everglade owned the
department store. He was Cassy's
boss and he was not a happy man.

"Go to my office," he yelled.
"NOW!"
Trembling, Cassy obeyed.

## Chapter 2

# A cross boss

Ernest Everglade was
furious. He liked salad,
but not on his head.

"Go and don't ever come back," he told Cassy. "I don't want a clumsy crocodile in my store."

Cassy begged and pleaded.
She pleaded and begged.
"Just give me one more
chance. I'll be very careful,"
she promised.

But Mr. Everglade was more
interested in his newspaper. He
wasn't even listening to Cassy.

At last, he looked up. "I don't have time for you," he sighed. "Some jewel thieves are in town, the famous Greedy Boys."

Cassy gasped. Everyone had heard of the Greedy Boys. But she still wanted her job back. She began to cry.

18

Now, Mr. Everglade couldn't stand crying. He would do anything to stop it.

"OK, OK," he said. "Go to the Luxury Goods Department first thing Monday morning."

Oh thank you! You won't regret it. I promise.

## Chapter 3

# Getting it right

The next day was Sunday.
Cassy worked hard at home,
getting ready
for Monday.

She emptied her cupboards and
stacked everything inside them.
She stacked every pot, plate, cup,
and saucer in the house.

The stacks got wobblier and
wobblier...

and higher...

and higher...

Next she found paper, scissors, ribbon and tape. She wrapped everything she could get her hands on.

When she'd finished wrapping, Cassy was exhausted. All she wanted to do was sit down.

But when she looked for her comfiest chair, there was just one small problem...

So she set up her mirror and
served imaginary customers.

"A flying pig? Try the pet
department sir... I'm sorry,
madam, we don't sell crocodile-
skin handbags."

"You don't like your spotted socks, sir? I'll change them at once."

And she smiled her toothy crocodile smile until her whole face ached.

Can I help you?

Finally, Cassy put on her
Everglades badge and admired
herself in the mirror. She
looked perfect!

## Chapter 4

# Cassy in charge

On Monday morning, Cassy
was the first to arrive in the
Luxury Goods Department.

Only the security guard was there. He had been guarding the store during the night.

The guard was finishing his breakfast. He was very pleased to see Cassy. Now he could go home to bed.

Cassy was nervous. She didn't want to be left alone in the store.

"You'll be fine," said the guard. "Just keep an eye on the Everglades Emerald."

The guard left. Cassy wasn't
nervous any more. She felt
important. She was in charge.

The Everglades Emerald was the most expensive thing in the store. It was kept in a case of extra strong glass.

Cassy thought it was the most beautiful jewel she had ever seen.

THE BIGGEST
EMERALD IN
THE WORLD

EXTRA STRONG GLASS

THE
EVERGLADES
EMERALD

35

But Cassy wasn't the only one admiring the emerald. Hiding behind a pot were Nigel and Rupert – the Greedy Boys!

"What a beauty," sighed Nigel.

"But look at that case," said
Rupert. "How will we ever
break the glass?"

"Never fear," Nigel whispered.
And as Cassy wandered away
from the emerald, Nigel took
something from his pocket.

# Chapter 5

# Disaster!

Nigel held up a small whistle.

"My secret weapon," he said.
"It can't be heard by humans,
but it can..."

He put the whistle to his lips
and blew. The case exploded.

"...shatter glass!" he finished.

He grinned. The Everglades
Emerald was theirs for the taking.

"At last," gasped Rupert. "I can't
wait to get my hands on it!"

Nigel and Rupert sneaked
out from their hiding place.
Their eyes glittered
with greed.

"Now to collect our prize,"
said Nigel.

The thieves crept closer to the emerald. But Nigel had made a big mistake.

He was right about humans not being able to hear his whistle. What he didn't know was that animals could hear it...

"Hey!" thought Cassy. "The
Toytown Express!" She spun
around, ready to race to the Toy
Department... forgetting her tail,
which swung around too.

This time it hooked a priceless
pearl necklace.

Cassy tugged her tail.

The necklace snapped, pearls
went everywhere and Cassy
went flying.

So did the Greedy Boys. The
rolling pearls sent them skidding
to the floor. They tumbled to the
ground, bringing the Everglades
Emerald with them.

Cassy turned to see the Greedy
Boys lying in a heap.

"Oh no! Customers!" she cried
and rushed over to help them up.

Rupert was groaning in agony. Nigel still had his eye on the emerald. He wouldn't let a clumsy crocodile ruin his plans. He'd waited years to steal this giant gem.

In her hurry to help, Cassy
tripped. She slid across the floor,
her arms thrust out...

and collided nose first with
a table, a table which held
Everglades' Ancient Treasures.

The table wobbled... the
treasures wobbled...

Then they crashed to the floor.

Cassy got up. She was horrified.
What had she done?

One of the ancient pots had
toppled off the table...

...straight onto her
customers' heads.

At that moment, the boss walked in. Cassy started to explain. But Mr. Everglade wasn't listening.

He had just seen the Everglades
Emerald lying on the floor.

Then he saw the pot. And the legs. And the bag lying next to them. And he quickly put two and two together.

He was no longer a cross boss. He was a very pleased and excited boss.

He picked up the emerald and beamed at Cassy.

"Well done! You've saved the Everglades Emerald."

Cassy was puzzled. Mr. Everglade pointed to the pot.

"And you've caught the Greedy Boys," he added.

"Oh? So I have!" said Cassy.

# Chapter 6

# Cassy the hero

That afternoon the boss
gave a party for Cassy.

The whole town was invited,
except for the Greedy Boys.
Nigel and Rupert were both
safely behind bars.

It was the best party ever.
There was singing and dancing,
cake and ice cream – and fantastic
fizzing fireworks.

Then Cassy was given a medal.
It was the proudest moment of
her life. She was a hero.

After the party, Mr. Everglade
smiled at Cassy.

"I've got a new job for you," he
said. He didn't want Cassy to be
an assistant anymore.

Instead, she became Everglades'
Chief Taster and Tester – with her
tail tucked firmly beneath her.

Try these other books in
**Series Two:**

**The Fairground Ghost:** When Jake
goes to the fair he wants a really
scary ride. But first, he has to teach
the fairground ghost a trick or two.

**The Incredible Present:** Lily gets
everything she's ever wished for... but
things don't turn out as she expects.

**Gulliver's Travels:** Gulliver sets sail
for adventure and finds a country
beyond his wildest dreams...

Series Editor: Lesley Sims

Designed by Katarina Dragoslavić
and Maria Wheatley